ROWAN AVA SKYE

The Axolotl and the Christmas Gift

Copyright © 2024 by Rowan ava Skye

All rights reserved. No part of this publication may be reproduced, stored or transmitted in any form or by any means, electronic, mechanical, photocopying, recording, scanning, or otherwise without written permission from the publisher. It is illegal to copy this book, post it to a website, or distribute it by any other means without permission.

This novel is entirely a work of fiction. The names, characters and incidents portrayed in it are the work of the author's imagination. Any resemblance to actual persons, living or dead, events or localities is entirely coincidental.

First edition

ISBN: 9798301788833

This book was professionally typeset on Reedsy. Find out more at reedsy.com

Contents

Introduction	1
Chapter 1: The Glittering Mystery	3
Chapter 2: The Riddle of the Reef	6
Chapter 3: The Shadow in the Deep	9
Chapter 4: The Jellyfish's Warning	12
Chapter 5: The Frozen Cavern	15
Chapter 6: A Wish for the World	18
Afterword	21

Introduction

Beneath the waves of the vast ocean, where sunlight danced on the surface and shadows whispered in the deep, there was a secret. It began on an ordinary evening in Ollie's quiet little cove, where the young axolotl was stacking tiny seashells into a tower that leaned far too dangerously to survive.

Crash! The tower toppled, scattering shells in every direction. Ollie sighed, scooping them up. "Maybe next time," he muttered, his voice barely louder than the bubbles floating around him.

But just as he was about to try again, a peculiar glow flickered in the distance. At first, Ollie thought it was a jellyfish—bioluminescent ones often wandered by. But this light was different. It pulsed, warm and golden, like a heartbeat.

"Strange..." Ollie swam closer, curiosity tingling in his fins. As he approached, the glow seemed to sense him. It shimmered brighter, almost inviting him.

Nestled between two rocks, half-buried in sand, was a small, mysterious object. It wasn't like anything Ollie had seen before. Round and smooth, it glowed with an unearthly light, and as Ollie touched it, warmth spread through him—comforting, yet somehow unsettling.

Before he could even wonder what it was, a whisper echoed in his mind. It wasn't a voice he recognized, but it spoke his name.

"Ollie..."

His gills fluttered as he looked around. No one was there. Only the object, glowing steadily in his hands.

"What are you?" Ollie whispered.

But the object didn't answer. Instead, its glow began to change, flashing faint patterns, as though it were alive. Then, as quickly as it had started, the light dimmed, leaving behind only a faint glimmer.

Ollie hesitated. Something about this object wasn't right. Yet he couldn't bring himself to leave it. Holding it close, he swam back to his cove, his mind racing with questions.

What was this strange thing? Why had it whispered his name? And why, deep in his chest, did he feel like this was only the beginning?

Little did Ollie know, the glow was far more than a mystery—it was a key. And unlocking its secrets would change everything.

Chapter 1: The Glittering Mystery

The glowing object pulsed faintly in Ollie's hands, casting a warm light that danced across the rocky walls of his underwater cove. It was unlike anything he had ever seen before. Round and smooth, it seemed almost alive, its golden light flickering in rhythmic patterns like the heartbeat of a sea creature.

"What are you?" Ollie murmured, holding it closer.

As if in response, the object grew warmer, sending a pleasant yet peculiar tingling sensation through his fins. Ollie shivered. He'd found treasures in the sand before—shiny shells, polished stones—but nothing as extraordinary as this.

Turning it over, he noticed faint markings etched into its surface. The lines formed swirling patterns, elegant and ancient, and at their center, a series of symbols glowed faintly.

"What does it mean?" he wondered aloud.

Just as he traced a finger along the inscriptions, the glowing object began to hum softly. The vibrations traveled up his arms, and then he heard it—whispers, faint and fleeting, like a breeze moving through kelp.

"Ol…lie…"

Ollie froze, his gills fluttering wildly. His name. The object had spoken his name.

"Who's there?" he called, glancing around the cove. There was no one else, only the steady pulse of the object in his hands.

The whispers grew louder, more insistent. **"Ollie… you must find the Light…"**

"The Light?" he repeated, his voice trembling. "What Light? What are you talking about?"

Suddenly, the object flared brightly, filling the cove with golden brilliance. Ollie squinted as the light etched new patterns into the walls, forming a strange map of symbols and shapes. It looked like a reef he vaguely recognized, but the glowing lines didn't stay still. They shifted, moved, and pulsed like a living thing.

In the center of the map, a single word appeared in bold, glowing letters. Ollie leaned closer, squinting to read it: **"Seek."**

His fins quivered as the whispers returned, clearer this time. **"You have been chosen... Find the Light before it is too late..."**

"Too late for what?" Ollie asked, panic creeping into his voice. But the light dimmed abruptly, plunging the cove back into the soft glow of the object.

For a long moment, Ollie simply floated there, staring at the mysterious item in his hands. He didn't know why, but his heart told him that this was more than just a treasure. It was a message, a call to something far greater than himself.

But why him? He was just a little axolotl. He wasn't brave or strong or clever. What could he possibly do that someone else couldn't?

The object pulsed again, softly this time, as though reassuring him. Ollie sighed and glanced at the map one last time. The glowing reef was just a short swim from his cove, a place he had visited many times.

"I guess I'm going," he said to himself, tucking the object into the pouch he wore around his neck. "Not like I have much of a choice."

As he left the safety of his cove, the ocean felt larger and quieter than usual, as if it too was holding its breath. The glowing object's whispers faded, replaced by a deep sense of unease. Ollie couldn't shake the feeling that someone—or something—was watching him.

The water grew colder as he swam toward the reef. Strange shadows shifted in the distance, and unfamiliar sounds echoed in the currents. Ollie tried to push down his fear, focusing instead on the object's soft, reassuring glow.

When he finally reached the Coral Reef of Secrets, it was eerily silent. Normally bustling with sea creatures and shimmering with life, the reef now seemed empty, its vibrant colors muted under the dim light of the ocean.

The object pulsed again, brighter this time, guiding Ollie to a small crevice nestled between two coral spires. As he peered inside, his breath caught.

There, etched into the stone wall, were the same swirling patterns he had seen on the object. The markings glowed faintly, as though waiting for him.

"This can't be a coincidence," Ollie whispered, pulling the object from his pouch.

As soon as he held it up, the patterns on the wall flared to life. The glowing lines spread outward, forming words in an ancient script that Ollie could somehow understand:

"The Light has been hidden for centuries. Its power is great, but its danger is greater. Only the pure of heart may seek it. Beware the darkness that follows…"

Ollie's fins tingled. Darkness? What darkness?

Before he could ponder further, the object's light grew blindingly bright, and for a brief moment, Ollie thought he saw something—a shadowy figure lurking just beyond the edge of the reef.

When the light faded, the figure was gone. But the words on the wall remained, glowing faintly in the dim water:

"Find the Light, or lose it forever."

Ollie swallowed hard, his determination wavering. He didn't understand what was happening, but one thing was clear—he had been pulled into something far bigger than he could imagine.

And somewhere in the darkness, something was watching, waiting.

Chapter 2: The Riddle of the Reef

The glowing object pulsed in Ollie's small, webbed hands, its light steady yet mesmerizing, casting shimmering reflections on the lagoon floor. It seemed to hum softly, a tune Ollie couldn't quite place but felt familiar, like a half-forgotten lullaby. The inscription etched on its surface—**"To find the Gift, you must first know its cost"**—echoed in his mind as he swam cautiously toward the Coral Reef of Secrets, a place whispered about in legends.

The Coral Reef of Secrets lay beyond the vibrant shallows Ollie called home. It was said to be a maze of twisting coral towers, vibrant but eerie, where sea creatures whispered truths they dared not speak above the waves. As he approached, the waters turned colder, and the colorful coral began to glow faintly, as if illuminated by an unseen moonlight.

"Who goes there?" a gravelly voice rasped from the shadows. A large grouper with cloudy eyes emerged, his fins lined with barnacles.

"I'm Ollie," he said, clutching the glowing object. "I need to know about the Lost Christmas Gift."

The grouper studied him silently before nodding toward a narrow crevice in the coral wall. "The keepers will decide if you are worthy."

Ollie squeezed through the gap, his heart pounding. On the other side, the reef opened into a stunning chamber filled with bioluminescent plants, their glow casting eerie patterns on the walls. Schools of translucent fish darted overhead like shooting stars. At the center of the chamber sat a ring of sea creatures—an ancient sea turtle, a shimmering angelfish, a prickly sea urchin, and a small but sharp-eyed crab.

CHAPTER 2: THE RIDDLE OF THE REEF

The sea turtle spoke first, her voice deep and resonant. "The Gift you seek is no ordinary treasure. It has brought joy to many, but despair to some. Do you know its purpose?"

Ollie shook his head. "I don't even know what it is! But this"—he held up the glowing object—"brought me here. It's leading me to the Gift. Can you help me?"

The angelfish swirled around him, her fins trailing like silk. "The Lost Christmas Gift," she said, her voice lilting, "is said to grant the deepest wish of the heart that finds it. But beware, little axolotl—wishes have consequences. The Gift's power has been hidden for a reason."

The crab clicked his claws impatiently. "Enough riddles! Tell him the story!"

The sea urchin, who had been silent, finally spoke, her voice as sharp as her spines. "Long ago, the Gift brought peace to the ocean. It brought light to the darkest depths and warmth to the coldest currents. But one day, a greedy shark found it and wished for endless power. The ocean turned on itself. Chaos reigned. That's why the Gift was hidden, protected by the Riddle of the Reef."

Ollie's heart sank. "If it caused so much trouble, why would anyone want it?"

The turtle's eyes gleamed. "Because the right hands could use it to bring back harmony. But if it falls into the wrong hands again…" She didn't finish the thought, but Ollie could imagine the destruction.

Before he could ask another question, the glowing object in his hands grew warmer, its hum rising in pitch. Suddenly, the chamber shook violently, and a dark shadow passed overhead. The coral walls dimmed as the creatures looked around in alarm.

"They've found us," whispered the angelfish, her shimmer dulling.

"Who?" Ollie asked, panic rising.

The crab scuttled toward him, shoving him toward an exit tunnel. "No time for questions, kid! You've got to keep moving!"

Ollie clutched the object tightly and swam as fast as his fins would carry him. Behind him, the shadow grew darker, its presence heavier. He heard the turtle's voice fading in the distance: "Remember the Riddle, Ollie. Know the cost!"

As he swam deeper into the twisting tunnels of the reef, the object grew cold in his hands, its hum shifting to a whisper. And then it spoke.

"Beware the one you trust the most."

Ollie stopped dead in his tracks, his heart pounding. "What does that mean?" he whispered, but the object offered no reply.

Above him, the shadow loomed closer, and Ollie realized with a chill that the danger wasn't just behind him. Someone he had yet to meet—someone he would trust—might betray him.

The thought clung to him as he swam onward, the cold weight of the object feeling heavier with every stroke.

Chapter 3: The Shadow in the Deep

The water around Ollie grew darker as he swam away from the Coral Reef of Secrets, the glowing object clutched tightly in his small hands. Its light, once bright and comforting, now flickered like a candle in the wind. He glanced over his shoulder, a chill running down his spine. The shadow was there again, lurking just at the edge of his vision.

It had appeared the moment he left the reef, a shape that didn't belong in the quiet, glimmering expanse of the open ocean. It wasn't a fish or a shark; it moved too fluidly, shifting in ways that made it seem almost formless. The shadow seemed to grow closer each time Ollie's heart raced, as though it could sense his fear.

"What do you want?" he whispered, but only the echo of his voice came back.

The glowing object in his hands grew colder, its light dimming further. It had whispered riddles before, but now it was silent, its warmth replaced by an icy chill that seeped into Ollie's fingers.

"I need you to help me," he pleaded, holding it up. "What am I supposed to do?"

The object pulsed weakly, and for a moment, Ollie thought it would answer. Instead, the shadow surged forward, blotting out the faint light entirely. Panic overtook him, and he darted into a thick forest of kelp, weaving through the swaying stalks in an attempt to lose his pursuer.

He stopped behind a dense patch, his gills fluttering as he tried to catch his breath. The shadow didn't follow immediately, but he could feel its presence—cold, heavy, and unrelenting.

"Why are you following me?" he called out. "I don't even know what I'm doing!"

To his surprise, the water around him seemed to shift, and a voice answered. It was deep and echoing, as if the ocean itself was speaking.

"You carry something that doesn't belong to you."

Ollie's eyes widened. "Who are you? What is this thing?"

The shadow didn't reply directly. Instead, it coalesced into a more defined form—a tall, imposing figure that resembled a manta ray, its wings gliding effortlessly through the water. Its body was made of swirling darkness, with glowing, piercing eyes that locked onto Ollie.

"It is not for you to know," the shadow said. "But it must be returned to where it came from. Hand it over."

Ollie shook his head, clutching the object tighter. "No! I don't even know what it is yet, but it brought me here for a reason. I can't just give it to you!"

The shadow surged closer, and the cold intensified. "Do you even understand what you're carrying? That thing will bring destruction if it falls into the wrong hands."

"And how do I know you're not the wrong hands?" Ollie shot back, his voice trembling.

For a moment, the shadow hesitated, its glowing eyes narrowing. Then it spoke, softer this time. "You don't. But there are others—others who will stop at nothing to take it from you. If you continue this journey, you won't just be hunted by me. You'll face dangers you can't imagine."

Ollie's mind raced. Was the shadow trying to help him or scare him into giving up the object? He wanted to trust the voice, but the glowing object suddenly pulsed with a faint warmth, as if warning him to stay cautious.

"I'm not giving up," he said firmly, swimming backward to keep distance between them. "If this thing is so important, I need to find out why."

The shadow let out a low, rumbling laugh. "Very well, little axolotl. But remember, the deeper you go, the darker it gets. And in the dark, you may not know who your real enemies are."

With that, the shadow dissolved, fading into the surrounding water as if it had never been there. But the cold lingered, and Ollie couldn't shake the

CHAPTER 3: THE SHADOW IN THE DEEP

feeling that it was still watching, waiting for him to falter.

As he swam onward, the glowing object brightened slightly, just enough to light his path. Its hum returned, faint but insistent, as if urging him to move faster.

But Ollie couldn't stop thinking about the shadow's words. Who were these "others" it had mentioned? Could he really trust the object he carried, or was it leading him into even greater danger?

Ahead of him, the water seemed to darken again, but this time it wasn't the shadow. The ocean floor dropped into an abyss, the edges lined with jagged rocks. The glowing object pulsed brighter, guiding him toward the inky blackness.

Ollie hesitated. "Into the deep?" he whispered.

The object answered with a single word, a whisper that sent shivers through him.

"Yes."

He glanced over his shoulder one last time, but the shadow was gone. Or so it seemed.

With a deep breath, Ollie swam forward, plunging into the abyss. As the darkness swallowed him, he couldn't help but feel that he wasn't alone—and that someone, or something, was waiting for him below.

Chapter 4: The Jellyfish's Warning

The Twilight Zone was a world unlike anything Ollie had ever seen. The sunlight no longer reached here, leaving the water bathed in dim, eerie shades of blue and gray. Strange creatures drifted in the shadows, their translucent bodies glowing faintly. It was silent except for the soft hum of the glowing object in Ollie's hands, its light casting long, shifting shadows across the ocean floor.

He shivered as a wave of cold water brushed past him, carrying with it an unsettling stillness. His heart pounded as he swam cautiously deeper, the object pulsing rhythmically, as if guiding him toward something—or someone.

"Who seeks the gift in the depths?" a voice suddenly echoed through the water, soft yet resonant, like the ringing of a distant bell.

Ollie froze, gripping the object tighter. "Who's there?" he called, his voice trembling.

A figure emerged from the darkness, its glowing body radiating a soft, golden light. It was a jellyfish, its bell-like head pulsating gently, and its long, flowing tentacles trailing behind it like strands of spun silk. The jellyfish's glow illuminated the surrounding water, revealing more of the mysterious creatures that hovered nearby, watching silently.

"You carry the Light of Wishes," the jellyfish said, its voice calm but filled with weight. "Do you know what it is you hold, little one?"

Ollie shook his head. "I don't. But it led me here, and I need to know why."

The jellyfish circled him slowly, its golden glow pulsing in time with the object in Ollie's hands. "The Light of Wishes is not merely an object. It is a

CHAPTER 4: THE JELLYFISH'S WARNING

key to a power older than the seas themselves. It holds the ability to grant a single wish to the one who completes its quest."

Ollie's eyes widened. "A wish? Any wish?"

"Any wish," the jellyfish confirmed. "But beware—such power is not given freely. The Light comes with a price, and not all who seek it understand the cost until it is too late."

The glowing object in Ollie's hands grew warmer, its hum growing louder. "What kind of cost?" Ollie asked, his voice a mixture of curiosity and fear.

The jellyfish paused, its glow dimming slightly. "The Light does not judge. It grants the deepest desire of the heart, but it does not choose wisely. Many who have sought it believed their wishes would bring happiness, only to find their desires twisted into something they could not control."

Ollie's gills fluttered as he processed the jellyfish's words. "So, it's dangerous?"

The jellyfish drifted closer, its tentacles swaying gently in the current. "It is not the Light that is dangerous, but the hearts of those who wield it. The ocean has seen kingdoms rise and fall because of the Light. Some used it to bring peace, others to create chaos. What will you wish for, little axolotl?"

"I don't know," Ollie admitted. "I didn't even know about the wish until now. I just... I thought I was supposed to find it."

The jellyfish tilted its bell-like head as if studying him. "Perhaps you were chosen for a reason. But you are not the only one seeking the Light."

Ollie's heart sank. "The shadow," he murmured. "And others, too. They're trying to take it."

The jellyfish's glow flickered, as if in warning. "Yes. The Light is coveted by many, and not all who seek it have noble intentions. The shadow you speak of is but one of many dangers. If you wish to complete the quest, you must prepare yourself for betrayal, for temptation, and for choices that will test the strength of your heart."

The glowing object in Ollie's hands pulsed sharply, almost as if in agreement. "But what happens if I don't finish the quest?" Ollie asked.

The jellyfish's light dimmed, casting long shadows over Ollie. "If the Light is left unclaimed, its power will fade, and the balance of the ocean will remain.

But if it falls into the wrong hands…"

The jellyfish didn't need to finish. Ollie could already imagine the chaos and destruction the shadow might unleash if it claimed the Light.

"I don't even know if I'm strong enough for this," Ollie admitted, his voice trembling.

The jellyfish's glow brightened slightly, like a reassuring smile. "Strength is not always about power, little one. Sometimes, the purest strength lies in kindness, in selflessness, and in the courage to make the right choice, even when it is the hardest one."

Before Ollie could respond, the water around them darkened suddenly, and the glowing object in his hands flickered wildly. The jellyfish straightened, its light flaring in alarm.

"They are close," it said, its voice urgent. "You must go, now!"

Ollie hesitated, but the jellyfish extended one glowing tentacle, gently nudging him forward. "Trust your heart, and remember my warning. The Light will test you, Ollie."

As he swam away, the glowing object in his hands seemed to guide him toward another path, its hum steady but insistent. Behind him, the jellyfish's golden glow faded into the distance, and the darkness of the Twilight Zone swallowed him once again.

But the jellyfish's final words lingered in his mind: **"Trust your heart. The Light will test you."**

And as the water grew colder and the shadows closed in, Ollie couldn't help but wonder—was he truly ready for the challenges ahead? Or would the Light of Wishes prove too powerful for him to control?

Chapter 5: The Frozen Cavern

The Arctic Cavern loomed ahead, its jagged walls of ice shimmering like diamonds in the faint glow of the object Ollie carried. He hesitated before entering, shivering from the freezing currents that flowed from the cavern's entrance. The glowing object was nearly blinding now, its light illuminating the path forward, but with each pulse, it grew colder in his hands, its chill biting through his skin.

He swam inside cautiously, his breath misting in the frigid water. The cavern walls were lined with crystalline ice, each shard reflecting the object's light like a thousand tiny mirrors. The air grew heavier, the silence oppressive.

"This must be the place," Ollie murmured, clutching the object tighter.

As if in response, the object pulsed brightly, its glow casting long, flickering shadows. Ollie felt a strange pull, as though the object were guiding him deeper into the icy labyrinth. But with each step, the temperature dropped further, and an eerie wind began to howl through the cavern.

A sudden snowstorm erupted, swirling around him with blinding force. Ollie shielded his face, trying to push forward, but the winds seemed determined to drive him back. "I won't give up now!" he shouted, his voice barely audible over the storm.

The glowing object flared brightly, cutting through the storm for a brief moment. But in the flickering light, Ollie saw it—a shadow darting across the cavern walls, growing larger with each pulse of the object's glow.

"Who's there?" Ollie called, his voice trembling.

The shadow didn't answer. Instead, it moved closer, its form shifting and growing until it towered over him. Suddenly, the storm stopped as abruptly as it had begun. The cavern fell into an icy silence, and the shadowy figure stepped into the light.

Ollie gasped, his heart pounding. The figure wasn't a monster or some formless being. It was... an axolotl.

But not just any axolotl. This one looked like him—eerily so. Its pale pink skin shimmered faintly, and its gills swayed gently in the water. But its eyes were darker, colder, and filled with an intensity that sent a shiver down Ollie's spine.

"Who... who are you?" Ollie stammered.

The shadow axolotl tilted its head, a slow, calculating smile spreading across its face. "You don't recognize me?" it asked, its voice smooth and unsettling. "I'm you, Ollie. Or rather, the part of you you've forgotten."

Ollie took a step back, shaking his head. "That's not possible. You're lying!"

The shadow axolotl chuckled, a low, echoing sound that seemed to fill the entire cavern. "Oh, but it is possible. You see, the Light of Wishes doesn't just grant desires. It reveals the truth—about the world, about others, and about yourself. And I am the truth you've been running from."

Ollie's grip on the glowing object tightened. "You're just trying to scare me. You're not real!"

The shadow axolotl stepped closer, its dark eyes locking onto Ollie's. "I'm as real as the wish you're chasing. Do you know why the Light chose you? Because your heart holds a wish so powerful, it created me. I am your doubts, your fears, your selfish desires. And unless you face me, you'll never be strong enough to complete the quest."

Ollie felt a surge of anger. "You don't know me! I'm not selfish, and I'm not afraid of you!"

The shadow axolotl's smile faded, its expression turning serious. "Oh, but you are afraid. Afraid of failing. Afraid of what the Light will reveal. You've been so focused on finding the wish, you haven't stopped to ask yourself what you'll do when you get it. Will you use it to help others? Or will you make a mistake like so many before you?"

The glowing object in Ollie's hands pulsed faintly, its warmth returning for just a moment. He looked down at it, then back at the shadow axolotl. "I

CHAPTER 5: THE FROZEN CAVERN

don't know what my wish is yet," he admitted, his voice shaking. "But I know I want to do what's right."

The shadow axolotl's eyes narrowed. "And how will you know what's right? The Light will grant your deepest desire, but it won't stop you from choosing wrong. That's why I'm here—to make you question everything."

Ollie took a deep breath, his resolve hardening. "Maybe I don't have all the answers yet, but I'm not going to let you stop me. The Light chose me for a reason, and I'm going to see this through."

The shadow axolotl's form began to flicker, its edges blurring like smoke caught in a current. "You're stronger than I expected," it said, its voice softer now. "But the hardest part of your journey is still ahead. Remember this, Ollie: the Light doesn't just test your courage. It tests your heart."

Before Ollie could respond, the shadow dissolved completely, leaving only the cold, empty cavern behind.

The glowing object in his hands flared brightly, lighting up a new path deeper into the cavern. Ollie hesitated, his mind racing with questions. Was the shadow right? Could he truly trust himself to make the right choice when the time came?

With a deep breath, he started forward. The path ahead was uncertain, but one thing was clear—his journey was far from over, and the greatest challenge was yet to come.

Chapter 6: A Wish for the World

Ollie emerged from the Frozen Cavern, the glowing object pulsing faintly in his hands. The cold still clung to him, but a new warmth radiated from the object as though urging him onward. The path had led him to the heart of the Arctic—a place where the ocean shimmered like glass under a brilliant, golden light.

In the center of the icy expanse stood an enormous crystal tree, its branches stretching toward the heavens, each one glistening with frozen droplets that refracted light in a rainbow of colors. At its base was a small pedestal, carved from ice and engraved with ancient symbols. Ollie instinctively knew what it was: the destination of his quest.

The glowing object in his hands pulsed brighter and hotter. As he stepped closer, it grew almost too brilliant to hold. He hesitated, suddenly aware of the weight of the moment.

"This is it," he whispered to himself. "The wish."

But before he could place the object on the pedestal, a voice echoed around him.

"You've done well to make it this far," said the shadowy axolotl, reappearing in the reflection of the crystal tree. "But now comes the hardest part."

Ollie clenched the object tighter. "I thought you were gone."

The shadow smiled faintly. "I am part of you, Ollie. I will always be here. And now, you must face your true test. What will you do with the Light?"

Ollie looked at the glowing object, his heart racing. For the first time, he could hear faint whispers emanating from it—voices of sea creatures, of children, of families. All of them were calling out, their wishes overlapping

CHAPTER 6: A WISH FOR THE WORLD

in a cacophony of hopes and dreams.

The shadow's voice softened. "You could keep it for yourself. After all, you've earned it. Your wish could bring you happiness, love, anything you've ever wanted."

Ollie frowned. "But the Light is meant to help others, isn't it? That's what the jellyfish said."

The shadow stepped closer, its dark form shimmering. "Helping others is noble, yes. But have you considered what you might lose by doing so? What if your wish was the one thing that could truly change your life? Do you want to sacrifice that for strangers?"

The question hung in the air, and Ollie felt his chest tighten. What did he want most in the world? For a brief moment, he thought of his small underwater cove, lonely on the quiet nights. He thought of his friends, their laughter filling the waters. A wish could change everything—it could bring him joy, companionship, or even a sense of belonging.

But then he thought of the voices. The sea creatures in the Coral Reef of Secrets, the wise jellyfish, and even the shadow's warnings. Each of them had reminded him of the power and danger of the Light.

Taking a deep breath, Ollie stepped toward the pedestal. The object in his hands burned brightly, its warmth filling his entire being. "I don't know what the right choice is," he said aloud, "but I know what feels right."

The shadow tilted its head. "And that is?"

Ollie placed the glowing object on the pedestal. The moment it touched the icy surface, the tree above exploded into radiant light, its branches glowing with a brilliance that illuminated the entire Arctic. The voices of wishes grew louder, swirling around him, until one voice rose above the rest—a deep, resonant tone that seemed to come from the tree itself.

"You have chosen to give," the voice said, echoing through the cavernous expanse. "The Light will be shared with the world."

Ollie's heart swelled with both pride and sadness. "What does that mean?" he asked.

The tree's light began to coalesce, forming a golden wave that spread outward in all directions. "It means the wishes of the world will be granted.

Joy will be shared. But the Light will no longer belong to you."

As the wave passed over him, Ollie felt a strange warmth envelop him. Memories of his journey flickered before his eyes—the Coral Reef of Secrets, the jellyfish, the shadow, and the Frozen Cavern. Each moment had brought him closer to this choice.

When the light faded, the glowing object was gone, and the tree stood quiet and still. The shadowy axolotl reappeared beside him, its expression unreadable.

"You gave it up," the shadow said. "Even though you could have kept it."

Ollie nodded. "It wasn't mine to keep. The world needed it more than I did."

The shadow regarded him for a long moment before smiling faintly. "Perhaps you've grown more than I thought."

As the shadow began to fade, Ollie called out, "Wait! What happens now?"

The shadow paused, its form flickering. "Now? Now, you go home, Ollie. And maybe one day, you'll understand that giving was the greatest wish of all."

With that, the shadow disappeared, leaving Ollie alone in the silent Arctic. He turned back toward the open ocean, a bittersweet smile on his face. Though the Light was gone, something else had taken its place—a sense of peace, of knowing he had done what was right.

And as he swam home, the world above and below began to glow with a new kind of magic—a Christmas Gift that would bring joy to everyone, everywhere.

Afterword

Dear Readers,

Thank you so much for joining Ollie on his magical journey in *The Axolotl and the Christmas Gift*. Your imagination and curiosity are what make stories like this come to life. We hope you felt the wonder, excitement, and joy that Ollie discovered along the way.

This tale may have ended, but Ollie's adventures—and many more enchanting stories—are just beginning! Keep an eye out for the next chapter in our holiday-themed series, where even more surprises, twists, and heartwarming moments await.

If you enjoyed this story, we invite you to explore our collection of books featuring other delightful tales of holidays and celebrations, perfect for sharing with family and friends. Whether it's a gift for a loved one or a cozy read for yourself, there's always something special waiting to be discovered.

From all of us, thank you for being part of this journey. Until next time, stay curious, stay kind, and keep the spirit of magic alive in your heart.

Warm wishes,

Rowan ava Skye

P.S. Don't forget to check out our other stories and characters—each one crafted to bring a little extra joy to your celebrations. Follow along as we continue creating magical tales to brighten every holiday season!

Printed in Great Britain
by Amazon